The JOY of Starting SCHOOL

THERESE BOBE BALCHAN

AuthorHouse™ UK
1663 Liberty Drive
Bloomington, IN 47403 USA
www.authorhouse.co.uk
UK TFN: 0800 0148641 (Toll Free inside the UK)
UK Local: 02036 956322 (+44 20 3695 6322 from outside the UK)

Because of the dynamic nature of the Internet, any web addresses or links contained in this book may have changed since publication and may no longer be valid. The views expressed in this work are solely those of the author and do not necessarily reflect the views of the publisher, and the publisher hereby disclaims any responsibility for them.

Any people depicted in stock imagery provided by Getty Images are models, and such images are being used for illustrative purposes only.
Certain stock imagery © Getty Images.

This book is printed on acid-free paper.

ISBN: 978-1-6655-9896-5 (sc)
ISBN: 978-1-6655-9895-8 (e)

Print information available on the last page.

Published by AuthorHouse 06/01/2022

authorHOUSE®

About the Author

My name is M. Therese Bobe-Balchan. I am a hardworking, honest person and a good listener. I am willing to learn new things. I am very friendly, a good time keeper and a great sense of humour. I adjust to change with ease. I have been a trained nurse for the past 38 years and have enjoyed it so much. I am dedicated and get across to people very well. Currently, I am looking forward to get my first book published. I am also a grandmother who cares for my 3 grandchildren aged under 18 years old.

My goal is continue writing books and that's my pleasure in achieving my dreams.

This is the house where Aaron lives with his mum and dad. Aaron is the only child of the family.

Today is sort of unusual in Aaron's house. It's the first day of school for Aaron. He has been really looking forward for this day.

Dad has left the house and gone to work at his office in the city. That morning Aaron woke up very early. He was so excited to go to school to meet his new teacher and classmates.

Mum prepared him by giving him a nice shower and help him with his school uniform.

Afterwards mum prepared his breakfast and got his packed lunch into his satchel.

Once they have got ready, they walked to the bus stop to get the bus to the school.

They could not go by car because his dad had to drive to his workplace. After few stops, they got off the bus, walk a short distance and arrived at the school.

Mum then, kissed and hugged Aaron and waved goodbye. Mum returned back home. She felt very sad and lonely without Aaron.

There were lots of children with their mums and dads waiting around.

Suddenly the bell started to ring and all the children lined up where their teachers were, ready to go in the classrooms.

That day passed so slowly and it seemed as if it's not going to end.

She missed Aaron being around but she had to take hold of herself and realized that Aaron was growing and he needed to be in school for an education and as time passed she might feel better on her own and have to find something to do to occupy her time while Aaron was at school.

At 3:15pm mum arrived at the school gate and after a short while the parents were allowed in the school ground to pick their children.

Mum couldn't wait to see Aaron to give him a big hug and asked him lots of questions about his first day.

When Aaron came out, he looked very happy.

Then they got on the bus home. Arriving home, mum emptied his satchel. Aaron got changed, washed his hands and mum gave him a snack and some milk.

His dad was pleased to know that Aaron would be settling well in his school.

"What and exciting day!" recalled Aaron.

>>>THE END<<<

Printed in the United States
by Baker & Taylor Publisher Services